I AM LOVE

A BOOK of COMPASSION

BY SUSAN VERDE · ART BY PETER H. REYNOLDS

Abrams Books for Young Readers · New York

The illustrations in this book were created using ink, gouache, watercolor, and tea.

Library of Congress Cataloging-in-Publication Data
Names: Verde, Susan, author. | Reynolds, Peter H. (Peter Hamilton), 1961- illustrator.
Title: I am love / by Susan Verde ; art by Peter H. Reynolds.
Description: New York, NY: Abrams Books for Young Readers, 2019. | Summary:
Explores many aspects of love that can help one weather any storm,
including that love is comfort, effort, connection, and taking care of oneself.
Identifiers: LCCN 2018058732 | ISBN 9781419737268
Subjects: | CYAC: Love—Fiction. | Conduct of life—Fiction.
Classification: LCC PZ7.1.V46 Iaael 2019 | DDC [E]—dc23

Printed and bound in U.S.A.
10 9 8 7

Abrams Books for Young Readers are available at special discounts when purchased in quantity for
premiums and promotions as well as fundraising or educational use. Special editions can also be
created to specification. For details, contact specialsales@abramsbooks.com or the address below.

Abrams® is a registered trademark of Harry N. Abrams, Inc.

ABRAMS The Art of Books
195 Broadway, New York, NY 10007
abramsbooks.com

This book is my love letter to the world,
as each one of us is worthy of love in all its forms and expressions,
and we are ALL capable of adding light to the world when we listen
to our hearts and choose love.
Love, S.V.

To my mother, Hazel Reynolds, the Queen of Love.
 P.H.R.

When I see someone going through a storm

of hurt and unfairness,
of anger and sadness...

when the sun disappears
and the skies grow dark...

I put my hands on my heart and listen.
And that is where I find the answer:

I have compassion.
I act with tenderness.

I am love.

I can listen and not say a word. I can be there.
Love is being present.

I can hug and hold and say, "Everything will be alright."
Love is comfort.

I can speak softly and choose my words and actions carefully. Love is gentle.

I can give thanks for all I have and am able to share.
Love is gratitude.

I can keep my mind and body safe and healthy.
Love is taking care of me.

I can express what's important to me.
Love is creative.

I can know that no one is perfect.
Love is understanding.

I can do my best to make things better
when something is wrong.
Love is effort.

I can celebrate those I've loved before.
Love is remembering.

I can find goodness in a kind word,
a helping hand, or a shared smile.
Love is tiny gestures.

I can breathe in the air that the whole world shares
and know all creatures are made from the very same stardust.
Love is connection.

When the clouds roll in, for others and for me,
I know now there is something I can do.

I can let my heart lead the way.

I am love.

You are love.

We are love.

And with love we will weather the storm
and light up the sky ...

together.

Author's Note

Love is everywhere! It is inside of us and all around us, and there are so many ways it can be shared and expressed. But sometimes things happen in life that make us feel afraid, sad, frightened, or helpless, and our ability to find that love can get lost. *I Am Love* is an exploration of the many ways love exists, and an affirmation of how—once we listen to our hearts and find the love within ourselves—we can share it with the world and find connection and compassion. My hope is that this book will inspire conversations with our children about love in all its expressions, and about how we are not helpless but in fact have the power to make the world more beautiful when we come from a place of love.

As a kids' yoga and mindfulness teacher, I often look to these practices to help children cope with the heavy emotions they feel. There are very simple exercises that children of all ages can do to positively affect their physiology and cultivate a sense of connection and compassion. Following are some heart-opening yoga poses and a simple heart meditation that can help body, mind, and spirit and bring forth love.

There is a lot of research showing that the way we carry ourselves is directly connected to our emotions and state of mind. When we see children hanging their heads or slouching, those can be signs that they are feeling unhappiness or anxiety and are trying to physically and emotionally protect their hearts. When your heart is closed off or "hurts," it is difficult to connect with others and to see, feel, or share love.

Heart-opening yoga poses allow us to literally lead with our hearts by opening and expanding the front of the body. These poses bring space and breath into the body and have been shown to positively affect mood and outlook and to create feelings of compassion and love. These activities can be done in school or at home, in any order, with others or alone, and they should be repeated a few times to fully experience the effects.

Heart-Opening Yoga Poses

Fish pose: Lie down on your back. Keep your legs straight and strong. Prop yourself up on your elbows with your palms on the floor and lift your chest and belly toward the sky, letting the top of your head rest gently on the floor. Feel your heart open as you breathe slowly through your nose into your heart space and belly. Tuck your chin and lower gently to the ground. If this feels too intense, a towel, sweatshirt, or blanket can be rolled and placed under the shoulder blades while lying on your back, arms resting on the floor, palms facing up. Even this slight lift under the rib cage can open the heart space.

Cobra pose: Lie on your belly, your legs straight and strong behind you. Place your palms flat on the ground next to your shoulders and draw your shoulder blades together on your back. Breathe in and gently push into the ground with your hands, keeping a slight bend in the arms, and lift your head, chest, and shoulders off the ground, aiming your heart to the sky. With each breath in, feel your heart expanding. Carefully lower yourself back down.

Cow pose in a chair: Kids of all ages spend a lot of time sitting, rounded over a desk or over electronics. This seated heart opener can be a wonderful break in the day that can also help with posture and spirit. Bring yourself to the edge of your chair and feel your feet on the ground. Reach back with both hands to either side of the seat of the chair. Inhale and lift your chest to the sky, arching your back. If it feels comfortable, let your head fall back gently as you widen your chest. Exhale and soften your posture. Inhale and repeat.

Heart Meditation

Now that these heart-opening poses have created physical space in the body, try this meditation to bring awareness and warmth into the emotional heart.

Find a comfortable seat and place your hands on your heart (or that space between your ribs known as your "heart space"). Placing a hand on your heart actually causes the release of a chemical in the brain called oxytocin, which, simply put, is the hormone of safety, bonding, and connection. This gesture can be extremely soothing to the nervous system.

Close your eyes or look down, and begin to breathe slowly in through your nose, directing your breath to your heart. Imagine with each breath that you are lighting up your heart with a warm, bright light. Notice how your heart feels.

As you continue to breathe, bring to mind a moment when you felt completely loved and safe. It could be a time shared with a parent, a pet, a teacher, a friend, or a kind gesture or word that made you feel that way . . . just a moment. Notice how your heart feels, and let that feeling travel through your whole body.

Holding on to that feeling, breathe in and think "I am love." Breathe out and think "I give love." Imagine the warmth and light in your heart connecting you to others in the world.

Do this for a few rounds of breath. Then slowly open your eyes and notice how you feel . . .

The more we do these practices, the easier it becomes to connect with our hearts and to find love, even when the clouds roll in.

Sending you love and light . . .